A GIFT FOR:

FROM:

BEDTIME STORIES II

*The Second Collection
of Calming Classics*

BEDTIME STORIES II

The Second Collection
of Calming Classics

A Division of HarperCollins*Publishers*

BOK 1062

Published under license from HarperCollins Publishers Inc.
www.harperchildrens.com
ISBN 0-06-095515-5
FIRST EDITION

10   9   8   7   6   5   4   3   2
❖

Contents

BEDTIME STORIES II

The Second Collection
of Calming Classics

Humpty Dumpty

Humpty Dumpty sat on a wall,
Humpty Dumpty had a great fall.
All the king's horses,
And all the king's men,
Couldn't put Humpty together again.

Mary Had a Little Lamb

Mary had a little lamb,
Its fleece was white as snow;
And everywhere that Mary went
The lamb was sure to go.

It followed her to school one day,
That was against the rule;
It made the children laugh and play
To see a lamb at school.

And so the teacher turned it out,
But still it lingered near,
And waited patiently about
Till Mary did appear.

Why does the lamb love Mary so?
The eager children cry;
Why, Mary loves the lamb, you know,
The teacher did reply.

3

To Market

To market, to market, to buy a fat pig,
Home again, home again, jiggety-jig;

To market, to market, to buy a fat hog,
Home again, home again, jiggety-jog.

The Queen of Hearts

The Queen of Hearts
She made some tarts,
All on a summer's day;
The Knave of Hearts
He stole the tarts,
And took them clean away.

The King of Hearts
Called for the tarts,
And beat the knave full sore;
The Knave of Hearts
Brought back the tarts,
And vowed he'd steal no more.

5

Bed in Summer

In winter I get up at night
And dress by yellow candlelight.
In summer, quite the other way,
I have to go to bed by day.

I have to go to bed and see
The birds still hopping on the tree,
Or hear the grown-up people's feet
Still going past me in the street.

And does it not seem hard to you,
When all the sky is clear and blue,
And I should like so much to play,
To have to go to bed by day?

Hot Cross Buns

Hot cross buns! Hot cross buns!
One a penny, two a penny,
Hot cross buns!
If you have no daughters
Give them to your sons;
One a penny, two a penny
Hot cross buns.

Going to St. Ives

As I was going to St. Ives,
I met a man with seven wives;
Each wife had seven sacks,
Each sack had seven cats,
Each cat had seven kits:
Kits, cats, sacks, and wives,
How many were there
    going to St. Ives?

One, Two, Buckle My Shoe

One, two,
Buckle my shoe;

Three, four,
Knock at the door;

Five, six,
Pick up sticks;

Seven, eight,
Lay them straight;

Nine, ten,
A good, fat hen;

Eleven, twelve,
Dig and delve;

Thirteen, fourteen,
Maids a-courting;

Fifteen, sixteen,
Maids in the kitchen;

Seventeen, eighteen,
Maids a-waiting;

Nineteen, twenty,
My plate's empty.

At the Seaside

When I was down beside the sea
A wooden spade they gave to me
To dig the sandy shore.

My holes were empty like a cup.
In every hole the sea came up,
  Till it could come no more.

Jack Sprat

Jack Sprat could eat no fat,
His wife could eat no lean;
And so betwixt them both you see,
They licked the platter clean.

Block City

What are you able to build with your blocks?
Castles and palaces, temples and docks.
Rain may keep raining, and others go roam,
But I can be happy and building at home.

Let the sofa be mountains, the carpet be sea,
There I'll establish a city for me:
A kirk and a mill and a palace beside,
And a harbor as well where my vessels may
　　ride.

Great is the palace with pillar and wall,
A sort of a tower on the top of it all,
And steps coming down in an orderly way
To where my toy vessels lie safe in the bay.

This one is sailing and that one is moored:
Hark to the song of the sailors on board!
And see, on the steps of my palace, the kings
Coming and going with presents and things!

Now I have done with it, down let it go!
All in a moment the town is laid low.
Block upon block lying scattered and free,
What is there left of my town by the sea?

Yet as I saw it, I see it again,
The kirk and the palace, the ships and the
    men,
And as long as I live and where'er I may be,
I'll always remember my town by the sea.

Rain

The rain is raining all around,
It falls on field and tree,
It rains on the umbrellas here,
And on the ships at sea.

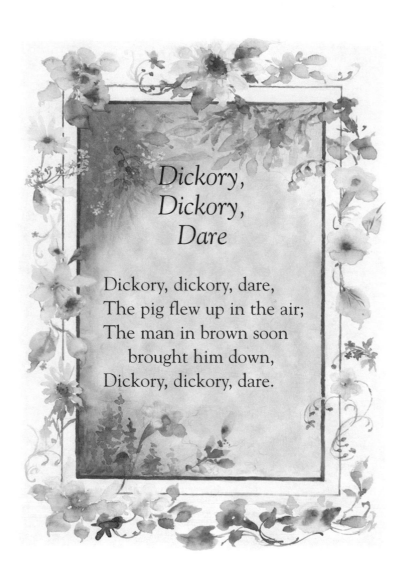

Dickory, Dickory, Dare

Dickory, dickory, dare,
The pig flew up in the air;
The man in brown soon
    brought him down,
Dickory, dickory, dare.

My Shadow

I have a little shadow that goes in and out
    with me,
And what can be the use of him is more than I
    can see.
He is very, very like me from the heels up to
    the head;
And I see him jump before me, when I jump
    into my bed.

The funniest thing about him is the way he
    likes to grow—
Not at all like proper children, which is always
    very slow;
For he sometimes shoots up taller like an
    india-rubber ball,
And he sometimes gets so little that there's
    none of him at all.

He hasn't got a notion of how children ought
to play,
And can only make a fool of me in every sort
of way.
He stays so close beside me, he's a coward you
can see;
I'd think shame to stick to nursie as that
shadow sticks to me!

One morning, very early, before the sun was
up,
I rose and found the shining dew on every
buttercup;
But my lazy little shadow, like an arrant
sleepyhead,
Had stayed at home behind me and was fast
asleep in bed.

Handy Pandy

Handy Pandy, Jack-a-dandy,
Loves plum cake and sugar candy.
He bought some at a grocer's shop,
And out he came, hop, hop, hop!

Peter Piper

Peter Piper picked a peck
    of pickled peppers;
A peck of pickled peppers
    Peter Piper picked.
If Peter Piper picked a peck
    of pickled peppers,
Where's the peck of pickled peppers
    Peter Piper picked?

Baa, Baa, Black Sheep

Baa, baa, black sheep,
Have you any wool?
Yes, sir, yes, sir,
Three bags full;
One for the master,
And one for the dame,
And one for the little boy
Who lives down the lane.

London Bridge

London Bridge is broken down,
Dance over my Lady Lee;
London Bridge is broken down,
With a gay lady.

How shall we build it up again?
Dance over my Lady Lee;
How shall we build it up again?
With a gay lady.

Build it up with silver and gold,
Dance over my Lady Lee;
Build it up with silver and gold,
With a gay lady.

Silver and gold will be stole away,
Dance over my Lady Lee;
Silver and gold will be stole away,
With a gay lady.

Build it up with iron and steel,
Dance over my Lady Lee;
Build it up with iron and steel,
With a gay lady.

Iron and steel will bend and bow,
Dance over my Lady Lee;
Iron and steel will bend and bow,
With a gay lady.

Build it up with wood and clay,
Dance over my Lady Lee;
Build it up with wood and clay,
With a gay lady.

Wood and clay will wash away,
Dance over my Lady Lee;
Wood and clay will wash away,
With a gay lady.

Build it up with stone so strong,
Dance over my Lady Lee;
Huzza! 'twill last for ages long,
With a gay lady.

Pat-a-Cake

Pat-a-cake, pat-a-cake, baker's man,
Bake me a cake as fast as you can;
Pat it and prick it, and mark it with B,
Put it in the oven for baby and me.

Diddle, Diddle, Dumpling

Diddle, diddle, dumpling,
　　my son John,
Went to bed
　　with his trousers on;
One shoe off,
　　and one shoe on,
Diddle, diddle, dumpling,
　　my son John.

Pirate Story

Three of us afloat in the meadow by the swing,
Three of us aboard in the basket on the lea.
Winds are in the air, they are blowing in the
    spring,
And waves are on the meadow like the waves
    there are at sea.

Where shall we adventure, today that we're
    afloat,
Wary of the weather and steering by a star?
Shall it be to Africa, a-steering of the boat,
To Providence, or Babylon, or off to Malabar?

Hi! But here's a squadron a-rowing on the
    sea—
Cattle on the meadow a-charging with a roar!
Quick, and we'll escape them, they're as mad
    as they can be,
The wicket is the harbor and the garden is the
    shore.

The Man in the Moon

The Man in the Moon came tumbling down,
And asked the way to Norwich;
He went by the south, and burnt his mouth
With eating cold pease porridge.

Pease Porridge

Pease porridge hot,
Pease porridge cold,
Pease porridge in the pot,
Nine days old.
Some like it hot,
Some like it cold,
Some like it in the pot,
Nine days old.

Old Mother Hubbard

Old Mother Hubbard
Went to the cupboard,
To give her poor dog a bone;
But when she got there
The cupboard was bare,
And so the poor dog had none.

She went to the baker's
To buy him some bread;
When she came back
The dog was dead.

She went to the undertaker's
To buy him a coffin;
When she got back
The dog was laughing.

35

She took a clean dish
To get him some tripe;
When she came back
He was smoking a pipe.

She went to the alehouse
To get him some beer;
When she came back
The dog sat in a chair.

She went to the tavern
For white wine and red;
When she came back
The dog stood on his head.

She went to the hatter's
To buy him a hat;
When she came back
He was feeding the cat.

She went to the barber's
To buy him a wig;
When she came back
He was dancing a jig.

She went to the fruiterer's
To buy him some fruit;
When she came back
He was playing the flute.

She went to the tailor's
To buy him a coat;
When she came back
He was riding a goat.

She went to the cobbler's
To buy him some shoes;
When she came back
He was reading the news.

Baby Bunting

Bye, baby bunting,
Daddy's gone a-hunting,
Gone to get a rabbit skin
To wrap the baby bunting in.

Little Miss Muffet

Little Miss Muffet
Sat on a tuffet,
Eating her curds and whey;
There came a big spider,
Who sat down beside her
And frightened Miss Muffet away.

Sing a Song of Sixpence

Sing a song of sixpence,
A pocket full of rye;
Four-and-twenty blackbirds
Baked in a pie!

When the pie was opened
The birds began to sing:
Was not that a dainty dish
To set before the king?

The king was in his counting-house,
Counting out his money;
The queen was in the parlor,
Eating bread and honey.

The maid was in the garden,
Hanging out the clothes;
When down came a blackbird
And snapped off her nose.

Little Jack Horner

Little Jack Horner
Sat in the corner,
Eating his Christmas pie;
He put in his thumb,
And pulled out a plum,
And said, "What a good boy am I!"

Bobby Shaftoe

Bobby Shaftoe's gone to sea,
Silver buckles on his knee;
He'll come back and marry me,
Pretty Bobby Shaftoe!

Bobby Shaftoe's fat and fair,
Combing down his yellow hair;
He's my love forevermore,
Pretty Bobby Shaftoe.

My Treasures

These nuts, that I keep in the
    back of the nest
Where all my lead soldiers are
    lying at rest,
Were gathered in autumn by
    nursie and me
In a wood with a well by the
    side of the sea.

This whistle we made (and how
    clearly it sounds!)
By the side of a field
    at the end of the grounds.

Of a branch of a plane, with a
    knife of my own,
It was nursie who made it, and
    nursie alone!

The stone, with the white and
    the yellow and gray,
We discovered I cannot tell *how*
    far away;
And I carried it back although
    weary and cold,
For though Father denies it, I'm
    sure it is gold.

But of all my treasures the last is
    the king,
For there's very few children
    possess such a thing;
And that is a chisel, both handle
    and blade,
Which a man who was really a
    carpenter made.

Jack and Jill

Jack and Jill went up the hill
To fetch a pail of water.
Jack fell down and broke his crown,
And Jill came tumbling after.

Then up Jack got and home did trot,
As fast as he could caper.
He went to bed and plastered his head
With vinegar and brown paper.

My Black Hen

Hickety, pickety, my black hen,
She lays eggs for gentlemen;
Gentlemen come every day
To see what my black hen doth lay.

The Swing

How do you like to go up in a swing,
Up in the air so blue?
Oh, I do think it the pleasantest thing
Ever a child can do!

Up in the air and over the wall,
Till I can see so wide,
Rivers and trees and cattle and all
Over the countryside—

Till I look down on the garden green,
Down on the roof so brown—
Up in the air I go flying again,
Up in the air and down!

What Are Little Boys Made Of?

What are little boys made of?
What are little boys made of?
Snakes and snails, and puppy-dogs' tails;
And that's what little boys are made of.

What Are
Little Girls
Made Of?

What are little girls made of?
What are little girls made of?
Sugar and spice
  and all that's nice;
And that's what little girls
  are made of.

The Land of Counterpane

When I was sick and lay abed,
I had two pillows at my head,
And all my toys beside me lay
To keep me happy all the day.

And sometimes for an hour or so
I watched my leaden soldiers go,
With different uniforms and drills,
Among the bedclothes, through the hills;

And sometimes sent my ships in fleets
All up and down among the sheets;
Or brought my trees and houses out,
And planted cities all about.

I was the giant great and still
That sits upon the pillow hill,
And sees before him, dale and plain,
The pleasant land of counterpane.

Diddlety,
Diddlety,
Dumpty

Diddlety, diddlety, dumpty,
The cat ran up the plum tree;
Half a crown
To fetch her down,
Diddlety, diddlety, dumpty.

Georgie Porgie

Georgie Porgie, pudding and pie,
Kissed the girls and made them cry.
When the boys came out to play,
Georgie Porgie ran away.

The Year

January brings the snow,
Makes our feet and fingers glow.

February brings the rain,
Thaws the frozen lake again.

March brings breezes loud and shrill,
Stirs the dancing daffodil.

April brings the primrose sweet,
Scatters daisies at our feet.

May brings flocks of pretty lambs,
Skipping by their fleecy dams.

June brings tulips, lilies, roses,
Fills the children's hands with posies.

Hot July brings cooling showers,
Apricots and gillyflowers.

August brings the sheaves of corn,
Then the harvest home is borne.

Warm September brings the fruit,
Sportsmen then begin to shoot.

Fresh October brings the pheasant,
then to gather nuts is pleasant.

Dull November brings the blast,
Then the leaves are whirling fast.

Chill December brings the sleet,
Blazing fire and Christmas treat.

Ride a
Cock-horse

Ride a cock-horse
    to Banbury Cross,
To see a fine lady
    upon a white horse;
Rings on her fingers
    and bells on her toes,
She shall have music
    wherever she goes.

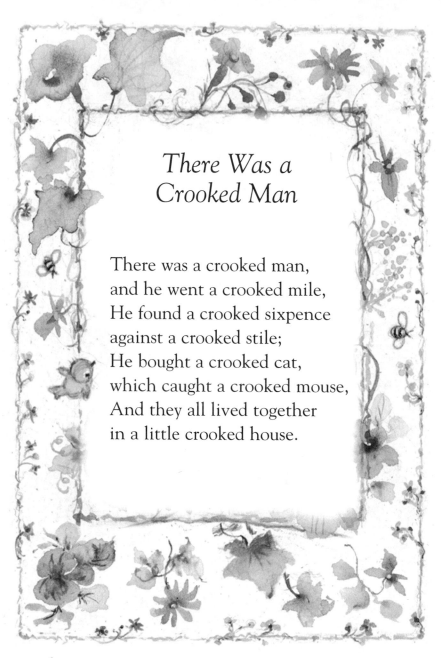

There Was a Crooked Man

There was a crooked man,
and he went a crooked mile,
He found a crooked sixpence
against a crooked stile;
He bought a crooked cat,
which caught a crooked mouse,
And they all lived together
in a little crooked house.

The Bunch of Blue Ribbons

Oh, dear, what can the matter be?
Oh, dear, what can the matter be?
Oh, dear, what can the matter be?
Johnny's so long at the fair.

He promised he'd buy me
   a bunch of blue ribbons,
He promised he'd buy me
   a bunch of blue ribbons,
He promised he'd buy me
   a bunch of blue ribbons,
To tie up my bonny brown hair.

My Bed Is a Boat

My bed is like a little boat;
Nurse helps me in when I embark;
She girds me in my sailor's coat
And starts me in the dark.

At night, I go on board and say
Good night to all my friends on shore;
I shut my eyes and sail away
And see and hear no more.

And sometimes things to bed I take,
As prudent sailors have to do;
Perhaps a slice of wedding cake,
Perhaps a toy or two.

All night across the dark we steer;
But when the day returns at last,
Safe in my room, beside the pier,
I find my vessel fast.

Pussy-cat

Pussy-cat, pussy-cat,
Where have you been?
I've been to London
To look at the Queen.
Pussy-cat, pussy-cat,
What did you there?
I frightened a little mouse
Under her chair.

The Cat and the Fiddle

Hey, diddle, diddle!
The cat and the fiddle,
The cow jumped over the moon;
The little dog laughed
To see such sport,
And the dish ran away with the spoon.

66

The Mulberry Bush

Here we go round the mulberry bush,
The mulberry bush, the mulberry bush,
Here we go round the mulberry bush,
On a cold and frosty morning.

This is the way we wash our hands,
Wash our hands, wash our hands,
This is the way we wash our hands,
On a cold and frosty morning.

This is the way we wash our clothes,
Wash our clothes, wash our clothes,
This is the way we wash our clothes,
On a cold and frosty morning.

This is the way we go to school,
Go to school, go to school,
This is the way we go to school,
On a cold and frosty morning.

This is the way we come out of school,
Come out of school, come out of school,
This is the way we come out of school,
On a cold and frosty morning.

Christmas Is Coming

Christmas is coming,
The geese are getting fat,
Please to put a penny
In the old man's hat.
If you haven't got a penny,
A ha'penny will do;
If you haven't got a ha'penny,
Then God bless you!

Ring-a-ring o' Roses

Ring-a-ring o' roses,
A pocket full of posies,
A-tishoo! A-tishoo!
We all fall down.

Thirty Days Hath September

Thirty days hath September,
April, June, and November;
February has twenty-eight alone.
All the rest have thirty-one,
Excepting leap-year, that's the time
When February's days are twenty-nine.

72

A Good Play

We built a ship upon the stairs
All made of the back-bedroom chairs,
And filled it full of sofa pillows
To go a-sailing on the billows.

We took a saw and several nails,
And water in the nursery pails;
And Tom said, "Let us also take
An apple and a slice of cake"—
Which was enough for Tom and me
To go a-sailing on, till tea.

We sailed along for days and days
And had the very best of plays;
But Tom fell out and hurt his knee,
So there was no one left but me.

Peter, Peter, Pumpkin Eater

Peter, Peter, pumpkin eater,
Had a wife and couldn't keep her;
He put her in a pumpkin shell,
And there he kept her very well.

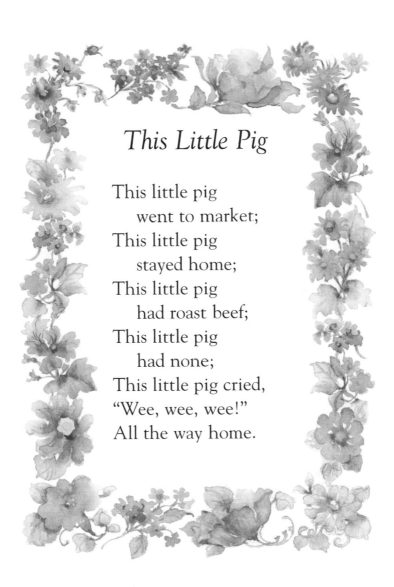

This Little Pig

This little pig
    went to market;
This little pig
    stayed home;
This little pig
    had roast beef;
This little pig
    had none;
This little pig cried,
"Wee, wee, wee!"
All the way home.

Three Little Kittens

Three little kittens
They lost their mittens,
And they began to cry,
Oh, Mother dear,
We sadly fear
Our mittens we have lost.
What! lost your mittens,
You naughty kittens!
Then you shall have no pie.
Mee-ow, mee-ow, mee-ow.
No, you shall have no pie.

The three little kittens
They found their mittens,
And they began to cry,
Oh, Mother dear,
See here, see here,
For we have found our mittens.

Put on your mittens,
You silly kittens,
And you shall have some pie,
Purr-r, purr-r, purr-r.
Oh, let us have some pie.

The three little kittens
Put on their mittens
And soon ate up the pie;

Oh, Mother dear,
We greatly fear
That we have soiled our mittens.
What! soiled your mittens,
You naughty kittens!
Then they began to sigh,
Mee-ow, mee-ow, mee-ow,
Then they began to sigh.

The three little kittens
They washed their mittens,
And hung them out to dry;
Oh, Mother dear,
Do you not hear,
That we have washed our mittens.
What! washed your mittens,
Then you're good kittens,
But I smell a rat close by.
Mee-ow, mee-ow, mee-ow,
We smell a rat close by.

Hickory, Dickory, Dock

Hickory, dickory, dock,
The mouse ran up the clock;
The clock struck one,
And down he run,
Hickory, dickory, dock!

The Little Girl with a Curl

There was a little girl and she had a little curl
Right in the middle of her forehead.
When she was good, she was very, very good,
But when she was bad she was horrid.

See-Saw, Margery Daw

See-saw, Margery Daw,
Jacky shall have a new master;
Jacky shall have but a penny a day,
Because he can't work any faster.

Little Bo-peep

Little Bo-peep has lost her sheep,
And can't tell where to find them;
Leave them alone, and they'll come home,
And bring their tails behind them.

Little Bo-peep fell fast asleep,
And dreamt she heard them bleating;
But when she awoke, she found it a joke,
For still they all were fleeting.

Then up she took her little crook,
Determined for to find them;
She found them indeed, but it made her
    heart bleed,
For they'd left all their tails behind 'em!

It happened one day, as Bo-peep did stray
Unto a meadow hard by—
There she espied their tails, side by side,
All hung on a tree to dry.

She heaved a sigh, and wiped her eye,
And over the hillocks she raced;
And tried what she could, as a shepherdess
    should,
That each tail should be properly placed.

The Seasons

Spring is showery, flowery, bowery;
Summer: hoppy, croppy, poppy;
Autumn: wheezy, sneezy, freezy;
Winter: slippy, drippy, nippy.

Great A, Little A

Great A, little a,
Bouncing B!
The cat's in the cupboard,
And can't see me.

The House that Jack Built

This is the house that Jack built.

This is the malt
That lay in the house that Jack built.

This is the rat
That ate the malt
That lay in the house that Jack built.

This is the cat
That killed the rat
That ate the malt
That lay in the house that Jack built.

This is the dog
That worried the cat
That killed the rat
That ate the malt
That lay in the house that Jack built.

This is the cow with the crumpled horn,
That tossed the dog
That worried the cat
That killed the rat
That ate the malt
That lay in the house that Jack built.

This is the maiden all forlorn,
That milked the cow with the crumpled horn,
That tossed the dog
That worried the cat
That killed the rat
That ate the malt
That lay in the house that Jack built.

This is the man all tattered and torn,
That kissed the maiden all forlorn,
That milked the cow with the crumpled horn,
That tossed the dog
That worried the cat
That killed the rat
That ate the malt
That lay in the house that Jack built.

This is the priest all shaven and shorn,
That married the man all tattered and torn,
That kissed the maiden all forlorn,
That milked the cow with the crumpled horn,
That tossed the dog
That worried the cat
That killed the rat
That ate the malt
That lay in the house that Jack built.

This is the cock that crowed in the morn,
That waked the priest all shaven and shorn,
That married the man all tattered and torn,
That kissed the maiden all forlorn,
That milked the cow with the crumpled horn,
That tossed the dog
That worried the cat
That killed the rat
That ate the malt
That lay in the house that Jack built.

This is the farmer sowing the corn,
That kept the cock that crowed in the morn,
That waked the priest all shaven and shorn,
That married the man all tattered and torn,
That kissed the maiden all forlorn,
That milked the cow with the crumpled horn,
That tossed the dog
That worried the cat
That killed the rat
That ate the malt
That lay in the house that Jack built.

Twinkle, Twinkle, Little Star

Twinkle, twinkle, little star,
How I wonder what you are!
Up above the world so high,
Like a diamond in the sky.

Ding, Dong, Bell

Ding, dong, bell!
Pussy's in the well!
Who put her in?
Little Johnny Green.
Who pulled her out?
Little Johnny Stout.

What a naughty boy was that
To try to drown poor pussy cat
Which never did him any harm,
But killed the mice in his father's barn!

One Misty, Moisty Morning

One misty, moisty morning,
When cloudy was the weather,
I chanced to meet an old man
Clothed all in leather.

He began to compliment,
And I began to grin,
How do you do, and how do you do,
And how do you do again?

Higglety, Pigglety

Higglety, pigglety, pop!
The dog has eaten the mop;
The pig's in a hurry,
The cat's in a flurry,
Higglety, pigglety, pop!

I Saw Three Ships
Come Sailing By

I saw three ships come sailing by,
Come sailing by, come sailing by,
I saw three ships come sailing by,
On New Year's Day in the morning.

And what do you think was in them then,
Was in them then, was in them then?
And what do you think was in them then,
On New Year's Day in the morning?

Three pretty girls were in them then,
Were in them then, were in them then,
Three pretty girls were in them then,
On New Year's Day in the morning.

One could whistle, and one could sing,
And one could play on the violin;
Such joy there was at my wedding,
On New Year's Day in the morning.

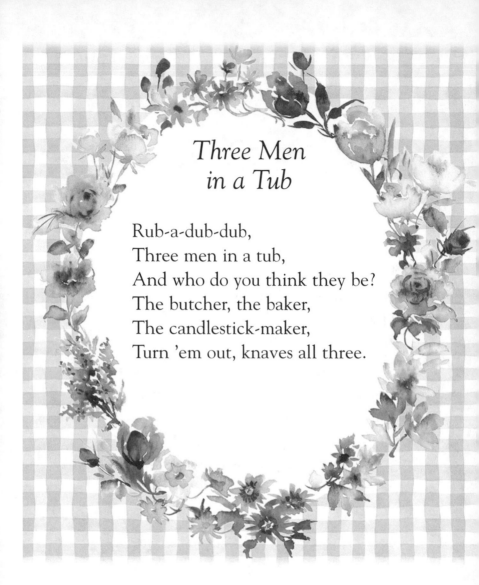

Three Men in a Tub

Rub-a-dub-dub,
Three men in a tub,
And who do you think they be?
The butcher, the baker,
The candlestick-maker,
Turn 'em out, knaves all three.

Hush-a-Bye, Baby

Hush-a-bye, baby, on the tree top,
When the wind blows, the cradle will rock;
When the bough breaks, the cradle will fall;
Down will come baby, cradle and all.

The Little Land

When at home alone I sit,
And am very tired of it,
I have just to shut my eyes
To go sailing through the skies—
To go sailing far away
To the pleasant Land of Play;
To the fairy land afar
Where the Little People are;
Where the clover tops are trees,
And the rain pools are the seas,
And the leaves, like little ships,
Sail about on tiny trips;
And above the daisy tree
    Through the grasses,
High o'erhead the Bumble Bee
    Hums and passes.

In that forest to and fro
I can wander, I can go;
See the spider and the fly,
And the ants go marching by,
Carrying parcels with their feet
Down the green and grassy street.
I can in the sorrel sit
Where the ladybird alit.
I can climb the jointed grass
    And on high
See the greater swallows pass
    In the sky,
And the round sun rolling by
Heeding no such things as I.

Through that forest I can pass
Till, as in a looking glass,
Humming fly and daisy tree
And my tiny self I see,
Painted very clear and neat
On the rain pool at my feet.
Should a leaflet come to land
Drifting near to where I stand,
Straight I'll board that tiny boat
Round the rain pool sea to float.

Little thoughtful creatures sit
On the grassy coasts of it;
Little things with lovely eyes
See me sailing with surprise.
Some are clad in armor green—
(These have sure to battle been!)—
Some are pied with ev'ry hue,
Black and crimson, gold and blue;
Some have wings and swift
   are gone—
But they all look kindly on.

When my eyes I once again
Open, and see all things plain:
High bare walls, great bare floor;
Great big knobs on drawer and door;
Great big people perched on chairs,
Stitching tucks and mending tears,
Each a hill that I could climb,
And talking nonsense all the time—
O dear me,
That I could be
A sailor on the rain pool sea,
A climber in the clover tree,
And just come back, a sleepyhead,
Late at night to go to bed.

I Had a Little
Nut Tree

I had a little nut tree; nothing would it bear,
But a silver nutmeg and a golden pear.
The King of Spain's daughter came to visit me,
And all was because of my little nut tree.
I skipped over water, I danced over sea,
And all the birds in the air couldn't catch me.

Mary, Mary, Quite Contrary

Mary, Mary, quite contrary,
How does your garden grow?
With silver bells and cockle shells,
And pretty maids all in a row.

There Was an Old Woman

There was an old woman
Lived under a hill,
And if she's not gone
She lives there still.

Little Robin Redbreast

Little Robin Redbreast sat upon a tree,
Up went Pussycat and down went he;
Down came Pussycat and away Robin ran;
Says little Robin Redbreast, "Catch me if you
can!"

Little Robin Redbreast jumped upon a wall;
Pussycat jumped after him, and almost had a fall.
Little Robin chirped and sang, and what did
Pussy say?
Pussycat said "Mew" and Robin jumped away.

The Moon

The moon has a face like the clock in the hall;
She shines on thieves on the garden wall,
On streets and field and harbor quays,
And birdies asleep in the forks of the trees.

The squalling cat and the squeaking mouse,
The howling dog by the door of the house,
The bat that lies in bed at noon,
All love to be out by the light of the moon.

But all of the things that belong to the day
Cuddle to sleep to be out of her way;
And flowers and children close their eyes
Till up in the morning the sun shall arise.

Little Boy Blue

Little Boy Blue,
Come blow your horn.
The sheep's in the meadow,
The cow's in the corn.
Where is the boy
That looks after the sheep?
He's under a haystack
Fast asleep.
Will you wake him?
No, not I,
For if I do,
He's sure to cry.

Simple Simon

Simple Simon met a pieman,
Going to the fair;
Says Simple Simon to the pieman,
"Let me taste your ware."

Says the pieman to Simple Simon,
"Show me first your penny."
Says Simple Simon to the pieman,
"Indeed, I have not any."

Simple Simon went a-fishing
For to catch a whale;
All the water he could find
Was in his mother's pail!

Simple Simon went to look
If plums grew on a thistle;
He pricked his fingers very much,
Which made poor Simon whistle.

He went to catch a dicky bird,
And thought he could not fail,
Because he had a little salt,
To put upon its tail.

He went for water with a sieve,
But soon it ran all through;
And now poor Simple Simon
Bids you all adieu.

Three Blind Mice

Three blind mice, see how they run!
They all ran after the farmer's wife,
Who cut off their tails with a carving knife,
Did you ever see such a thing in your life,
As three blind mice?

The Old Woman
Who Lived in a Shoe

There was an old woman
who lived in a shoe;
She had so many children
she didn't know what to do.
She gave them some broth
without any bread;
Then whipped them
all soundly and put them
to bed.

Tom, Tom, the Piper's Son

Tom, Tom, the Piper's son,
Stole a pig, and away he run.
The pig was eat, and Tom was beat,
And Tom went crying down the street.

This Is the Way

This is the way the ladies ride,
Tri, tre, tre, tree,
Tri, tre, tre, tree!
This is the way the ladies ride,
Tri, tre, tre, tre, tri-tre-tre-tree!

This is the way the gentlemen ride,
Gallop-a-trot,
Gallop-a-trot!
This is the way the gentlemen ride,
Gallop-a-gallop-a-trot!

This is the way the farmers ride,
Hobbledy-hoy,
Hobbledy-hoy!
This is the way the farmers ride,
Hobbledy-hobbledy-hoy!

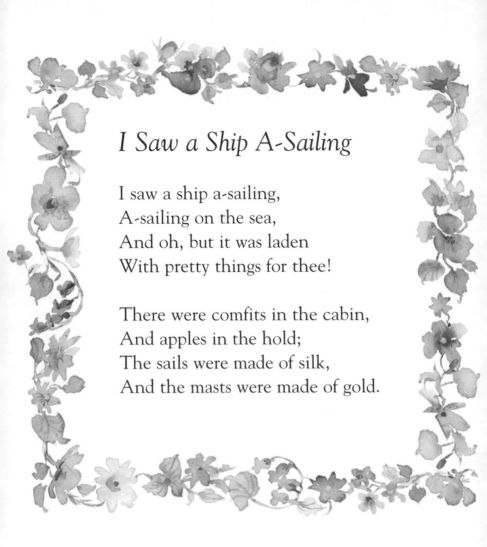

I Saw a Ship A-Sailing

I saw a ship a-sailing,
A-sailing on the sea,
And oh, but it was laden
With pretty things for thee!

There were comfits in the cabin,
And apples in the hold;
The sails were made of silk,
And the masts were made of gold.

The four-and-twenty sailors,
That stood between the decks,
Were four-and-twenty white mice
With chains about their necks.

The captain was a duck
With a packet on his back,
And when the ship began to move
The captain said, Quack! Quack!

Little Bird

Once I saw a little bird
Come hop, hop, hop;
So I cried, "Little bird,
Will you stop, stop, stop?"

I was going to the window
To say, "How do you do?"
But he shook his little tail,
And away he flew.

Old
King Cole

Old King Cole
Was a merry old soul,
And a merry old soul was he;
He called for his pipe,
And he called for his bowl,
And he called for his fiddlers three.

Every fiddler, he had a fiddle,
And a very fine fiddle had he;
Twee tweedle dee, tweedle dee, went
    the fiddlers.
Oh, there's none so rare
As can compare
With King Cole and his fiddlers three.

Marching Song

Bring the comb and play upon it!
Marching, here we come!
Willie cocks his highland bonnet,
Johnnie beats the drum.

Mary Jane commands the party,
Peter leads the rear;
Feet in time, alert and hearty,
Each a grenadier!

All in the most martial manner
Marching double-quick;
While the napkin, like a banner,
Waves upon the stick!

Here's enough of fame and pillage,
Great commander Jane!
Now that we've been round the village,
Let's go home again.

Ride Away,
Ride Away

Ride away, ride away,
Johnny shall ride,
And he shall have pussycat
Tied to one side;
And he shall have little dog
Tied to the other,
And Johnny shall ride
To see his grandmother.

Two Birds

There were two birds sat on a stone,
Fa, la, la, la, lal, de;
One flew away, and then there was one,
Fa, la, la, la, lal, de;
The other bird flew after,
And then there was none,
Fa, la, la, la, lal, de;
And so the stone
Was left alone,
Fa, la, la, la, lal, de.

Jack Be Nimble

Jack be nimble,
Jack be quick,
Jack jump over
The candlestick.

Monday's Child

Monday's child is fair of face,
Tuesday's child is full of grace,
Wednesday's child is full of woe,
Thursday's child has far to go,
Friday's child is loving and giving,
Saturday's child works hard for its living,
But the child that's born on the Sabbath day
Is bonny and blithe, and good and gay.

Young Night-Thought

All night long and every night,
When my mama puts out the light,
I see the people marching by,
As plain as day, before my eye.

Armies and emperors and kings,
All carrying different kinds of things,
And marching in so grand a way,
You never saw the like by day.

So fine a show was never seen
At the great circus on the green;
For every kind of beast and man
Is marching in that caravan.

At first they move a little slow,
But still the faster on they go,
And still beside them close I keep
Until we reach the town of Sleep.

Wee Willie Winkie

Wee Willie Winkie runs through the town,
Upstairs and downstairs in his nightgown,
Rapping at the window, crying through the
   lock,
"Are the children all in bed, for now it's eight
   o'clock?"